Angel of the Alamo

~ A True Story of Texas ~

by Lisa Waller Rogers

Illustrated by Gwen Thigpen

෧෨

W. S. Benson & Co.

Austin

To Tom and Katie

To Jerry, Erika, Catina, Kellon & Jerry
Thanks, Charlotte

Copyright © 2000 Lisa Waller Rogers

Published in the United States of America
by W.S. Benson & Company, Inc., P.O. Box 1866, Austin, Texas 78767

ISBN: 0-87443-125-5 Hardback   ISBN: 0-87443-126-3 Paperback

Library of Congress Cataloging-in-Publication Data
1. Villanueva, Andrea Castañón, 1803-1899–Juvenile biography. 2. Alamo (San Antonio, Tex.)–Siege, 1836–Juvenile fiction. [1. Villanueva, Andrea Castañón, 1803-1899–Biography. 2. Alamo (San Antonio, Tex.)–Siege, 1836–Fiction.] I. Title.
PZ7.R884An
[Fic]

If a man is called to be a streetsweeper,

he should sweep streets

even as Michelangelo painted,

or Beethoven composed music,

or Shakespeare wrote poetry.

He should sweep streets so well

that all the hosts of heaven and earth

will pause to say,

"Here lived a great streetsweeper

who did his job well."

Dr. Martin Luther King, Jr.

he desert simply crawls with danger. It is no place for a baby. But try telling that to Andrea. Because the desert is exactly where she decided to be born.

It was dark that night. Andrea's parents, Jóse and Francisca, were sleeping on the riverbanks of the Río Grande. Since sunrise, they had been walking. They were traveling with other settlers to Laredo.

Francisca's back ached. She was expecting a child. Exhausted, they had all stopped for the night and pitched camp. Francisca had just dozed off when she felt the earth rumble beneath her. "José…" she said, "José!" She shook him hard. "EARTHQUAKE!"

Earthquake? José pressed his ear to the ground. This was no earthquake! A mob of horses was galloping their way!

"APACHE ATTACK!" he shouted. The other settlers sprang to attention. José barked orders. "Shake the bushes! Clap your hands! Stamp your feet! Fire your guns!"

They made a terrible commotion. In fact, they were so noisy, they almost missed hearing the attackers ride away. The darkness had helped them trick the Indians into believing there were too many of them to beat. "Hooray!" cheered everyone, except Francisca, who was nowhere in sight.

Way out on the edge of the campsite, behind some tall grasses, Francisca had just given birth to a baby girl.

"Because today is St. Andrew's Day," she whispered to her baby, "I name you Andrea." Her child was surely blessed. In danger Andrea was born and in danger she would live.

☙℘

Once in Laredo, Andrea's parents built a hut of mud, sticks, and grass. This crude shelter wasn't much to look at, but, to them, it was home.

As Andrea grew older, the villagers saw she was no ordinary child. "What bright eyes she has!" they remarked. "What a lively tongue!" They marveled at her energy. She took to the desert like a jackrabbit, darting in and out of the cactus on bare feet. She floated above danger – like an angel.

Andrea stopped running to watch the curanderas – the folk healers of her people. They searched the desert for herbs, berries, and roots to use in their healing potions.

Andrea loved to watch a curandera at work. A curandera was a nurse, bandaging a scraped knee. Or, a curandera was a priest, saying prayers over the sick. Yet, a curandera was also a "mom," brewing peppermint tea for a fussy child.

Tea wasn't the only thing brewing in Laredo in 1810. Trouble was brewing. For months, it had not rained. Corn plants had shriveled up. With no corn, what were José and the other Mexican farmers to do? No corn meant no tortillas. No corn crop to sell meant no money. The poor Mexicans were starving.

At that time, the King of Spain ruled over Mexico. The starving Mexicans cried to him for help. He ignored them. Or, perhaps, he did not even hear their cries. After all, he did live thousands of miles away, across the ocean.

Frustrated, the poor Mexicans took action. Mexico should be ruled by Mexicans, they felt. They planned to overthrow the Spanish government. The cry of these rebels became "Long Live Independence!" They made bold speeches in the town square.

"Down with the bad government!" they cried.

When rich Spanish landowners heard the rebels putting down their king, they became furious. They sent their allies, the Spanish army, to crush the rebellion. Bloody fights broke out. People were killed. "This is no place to raise a family," said José.

So he loaded their few possessions onto a cart and hitched up the burro. José, Francisca, and Andrea headed east on the King's Highway. They would make a new life in San Antonio, a town 150 miles away from the fighting. Or, so they thought.

☙

For most of the trip, the scenery was what Andrea had always known: cactus, yucca, ocotillo, wiry grass, and shrubby mesquite. She grew restless. "Are we there yet?" she kept asking her mother.

"A little longer, dear," was Francisca's gentle reply. " Be patient, like the burro."

They slept under the stars and crossed many rivers. Every so often, a roadrunner zipped ahead of their cart before darting into the brush.

Then, a few miles north of the Medina River, the road led them to the top of a hill. Stretched out before them lay a broad, emerald valley.

"Look!" exclaimed Andrea.

"It reminds me of a city in southern Spain!" said José.

San Antonio looked like a city of white marble. Cream-colored houses clustered around a milky-green river. A cathedral dome towered over the town like a fat queen surveying her kingdom. Her cross caught a sunbeam. It flashed the immigrants a welcoming wink. Francisca smiled. "This omen is good," she said. She prodded the burro. They descended the slope into town.

15

After passing through some Chinese lilacs and crossing a creek, they entered the poor neighborhood of the barrio. An old woman squatted at a flat rock, rolling out tamales. Two boys raced past them, chasing a squawking chicken.

They then entered the town square, or plaza, which was framed by adobe houses. All were little and plain – except for one, the Spanish Governor's Palace. Over its huge, walnut doors was a double-headed eagle – a symbol of wealth and power.

"Who lives there?" exclaimed Andrea, staring. She would find out soon enough.

To the north, a muletrain carrying American soap to Mexico was lined up. It stretched so far east that Andrea could not see the end. Nearby, the mule driver leaned against a post, resting for the long journey ahead. His forehead dripped with sweat.

He mopped his forehead with a bandanna. Cupping his hands around his mouth, he shouted, "¡Ándale! ¡Ándale!" With his boot, he pushed away from the post and walked over to the lead mules. He slapped their bottoms. Slowly, the muletrain began to move out. The plaza swirled with dust.

In the center of the plaza, shoppers bought peaches from covered carts. In the shadow of the cathedral dome, an Apache sold leopard skins to a tanner. A chihuahua lazed in the sun.

The bells of San Fernando tolled mass. San Antonio seemed so calm.

☍☌

Once they were settled, Andrea became a companion to Gertrudis Cordero. She was the wife of the Spanish governor. They lived in the fancy Spanish Governor's Palace!

Andrea's first job was to make the Corderos' favorite drink – chocolate. She learned to spin the beater until the chocolate was just right – thick and foamy.

Being important people, the Corderos often entertained big groups. So Andrea learned how to prepare enormous feasts. Her cooking was so delicious that guests followed her into the kitchen asking, "Would you give me your recipe?"

Gertrudis liked Andrea. She took her along when, in her husband's absence, she reviewed the troops on Military Plaza. Wearing a dark-green, velvet riding suit and a plumed hat, Gertrudis rode sidesaddle, head high.

"She looked as grand as Queen Isabella!" Andrea told her mother later.

Indeed, Gertrudis was rich and beautiful. But what truly impressed Andrea was her kindness. With a basketful of food and a purse full of money, Gertrudis visited the sick and needy every Saturday. Like the curanderas, Gertrudis was an Angel of Mercy. Andrea wanted to become one, too.

Then, on a hot August day in 1813, the peace of San Antonio was shattered. Spanish troops swept through the city. They executed three hundred men suspected of being rebels. Afterwards, they locked up the Mexican women and girls of the city, including Andrea.

The women were forced to make ten thousand tortillas a day for the soldiers. Day in, day out, Andrea crouched, pounding corn into meal. Her palms and knees were raw and bleeding. Hovering over her was a brutal guard with a long whip. Andrea would never forget him.

Andrea whispered to the woman kneeling beside her, "Who is he?" The woman swallowed hard. "He is Lieutenant Antonio López de Santa Anna," she said. "SSSSHHHH!"

After several weeks, the hated troops freed the women and left the city. The experience changed Andrea forever. "From this day forth," she pledged, "I will help anyone struggling for freedom!" Like Gertrudis and the curanderas of Laredo, she would become an Angel of Mercy – no matter what the danger to herself.

In 1821, Mexico won its independence from Spain. It opened its Texas borders and invited Americans to fill up the land. San Antonio grew.

Andrea had become a beautiful woman. Although many men had tried to win her heart, she only had eyes for one man. He was the handsome and brave soldier, Candelario. They fell madly in love and were married.

With so many immigrants passing through San Antonio, Andrea and Candelario decided to open a restaurant. "Andrea's Place" was an instant hit. Andrea's enchiladas became famous.

The years flew by. The days of "bad government" seemed to be in the past. Andrea stayed busy with customers and her four children.

Then, in 1835, the Mexican government began acting dangerously. Mexico had a new president – General Antonio López de Santa Anna! He was the same Santa Anna who had invaded San Antonio twenty-two years before! Santa Anna was suspicious of Texans and their democratic ideas. They might try to overthrow him. He decided to show them who was boss.

That fall, General Cós, 1,200 Mexican soldiers, and 21 big guns rolled into San Antonio. They took over the city. Cós had orders to throw out any Americans who had come to Texas after 1830, collect all guns, and arrest anyone suspected of opposing Santa Anna. Recklessly, the army moved through town.

Citizens gathered at Andrea's to exchange damage reports.

"Three soldiers ripped up my floor and stole my grandmother's pearls!" said one woman.

"They broke into my store," said the grocer, "smashing pickle barrels and emptying flour sacks onto the counter!"

A lawyer arrived at his office to find his legal files burned to ashes. "Gone are my books, my maps, my land records! How can I ever replace those?" he asked.

Everyone asked, "Is there anyone who can stop this madness?"

There was. He was Colonel Jim Bowie, the adventurer. He and his scouts rode out into the countryside and issued a call-to-arms.

About 360 loyal Texans dropped what they were doing to join the fight. Armed with muskets, shotguns, Kentucky long rifles, and Bowie knives, these volunteers gathered in a field north of San Antonio. They plotted their attack.

After two months of waiting, Colonel Milam asked his Texan army, "Who will come with old Ben Milam into San Antonio?"

The Texans replied, "We will!" and stormed the city. For five cold, wet days and nights, the fighting raged from street to street and from house to house. The Texan soldiers were outnumbered, untrained, and lightly armed. But they never gave up.

Finally, General Cós surrendered. The Mexican army retreated.

The Texans were jubilant. They were also half-starved, homeless, dirty, sick, and wounded. Nothing Andrea could not help.

Over 250 soldiers poured into Andrea's Place. Out in front, they dropped their bedrolls and saddles and lined up for a plate of enchiladas.

Andrea was a blur of action. Like an Angel of Mercy, she cleaned wounds, had a kind word for everyone, and still managed to keep the food coming. She spent her own money to buy the soldiers medicine, supplies, and food. If Santa Anna found out she was helping the Texas cause, Andrea would pay with her life. Come what may, she had thrown in her lot with the rebels.

When General Cós fled San Antonio, he set fire to the only fortress, the Alamo. It was a blackened shell. It would need months of repair to be ready when Santa Anna arrived for his revenge.

In January of 1836, less than two hundred Texans were on hand to rebuild the Alamo. Under the command of Colonel Bowie, the men dug trenches and patched walls. They stopped only to eat the meals Andrea carted across the river each day.

Bowie told Andrea she was working too hard.

"The men have to eat to keep up their strength," she explained. "We can't expect them to work, fight, and cook."

Bowie kept a sharp lookout for other volunteers to arrive. To properly defend the three-acre fort, 850 men were needed. Any day, he expected to see Colonel Jim Fannin and his four hundred men arriving from Goliad. Yet it was not Fannin who arrived next, but Davy Crockett and his twelve Tennessee Mountain Boys.

"We've come to get a belly-full of fighting!" said Crockett. Everyone had heard of Davy Crockett, an expert shot with a rifle. To welcome him, the crowd piled up bonfires in the street. Crockett gave a rousing speech. Everyone cheered.

Afterwards, everyone gathered at Andrea's Place. Crockett played the fiddle and told tales of wild bears.

Colonel William Barrett Travis, who shared the command with Bowie, asked Crockett to defend the weakest Alamo wall. Crockett accepted.

In mid-February, Bowie's scouts reported that bakeries along the Rio Grande were baking enough bread for an army. Shortly afterward, Santa Anna was spotted in Laredo.

Santa Anna is coming! People began leaving San Antonio in caravans.

But Andrea was not leaving. She had been given an official duty. A letter had arrived at her home from General Sam Houston, her old friend and the commander-in-chief of the Texas army. It said:

Candelarita, (his pet name for Andrea)
Go and take care of Bowie,
my brother, in the Alamo.
Houston

Andrea had rushed to the Alamo. She had found Bowie lying on a cot, gravely ill with pneumonia. He was as white as a sheet. It was hard to believe that this was the same man who had once fought for his life against a hundred Indians for thirteen hours. Now he had only enough strength to say a few words. He had been forced to give up his Alamo command.

From then on, Andrea stayed by Bowie's side. She left only to run brief errands in town.

It was on one of those trips into town that Andrea saw a suspicious man lurking beside the road. He was driving a mule and selling hay. Andrea had never seen him before. He must have felt her stare because, right then, he looked up. She gasped.

"Santa Anna!" she thought to herself. He was plotting the invasion himself – in disguise! She hurried into town to spread the alarm – *Santa Anna is coming!*

It was just after noon on February 23 when the bells of San Fernando Cathedral began to clang frantically. A Texan scout had spotted the Mexican army marching from the Medina River. *Santa Anna is coming!*

Colonel Travis yelled, "Withdraw immediately into the Alamo!"

Citizens and soldiers raced across the river. They had barely barred the Alamo gates before hundreds of Mexican soldiers spilled into the plaza. Their lances, sabres, and bayonets gleamed in the weak winter sunlight.

General Santa Anna rode in on a horse with a gold-plated saddle.
He dismounted, tossing the reins to an underling. He strutted across
the plaza. He looked to the northeast. He saw a most unusual flag flying
over the Alamo. It was a Mexican flag, yet along with the red, white,
and green blocks was painted the date, 1824, in huge black numbers.

"How dare they!" thought Santa Anna. 1824 meant the Mexican Con-
stitution of 1824. It guaranteed settlers' rights. Santa Anna had done
away with those laws. The Texans were fighting to get them back.

Santa Anna had not expected this opposition. He would force their surrender. "Run up the red flag!" he ordered.

Colonel Travis, watching from the Alamo, saw the blood-red flag being raised over San Fernando Cathedral. Santa Anna was sending him a message: "Surrender at once or we will show no mercy!"

Travis was quick to reply. He fired his eighteen-pound cannon. BOOM!

"I shall never surrender or retreat. VICTORY OR DEATH!" vowed Travis.

The battle was on.

For the next twelve days, the crack of gunfire remained steady on both sides. Mexican cannonballs pelted the walls of the Alamo room where Andrea nursed Bowie.

34

At first, Bowie would leave his sick bed occasionally to check on the troops. Soon, though, his fever jumped so high that he did not even recognize his old friend, Juan Seguin. He couldn't get out of the bed anymore. He was dying.

Even so, he continued to fight. "Raise me up to the window," he told Andrea. Crockett loaded his pistols. With Andrea holding him up, Bowie would aim, fire, and fall back to rest.

With each passing day, it became doubtful that Fannin was coming. Although thirty-two men from Gonzales did arrive, Fannin never did.

Meanwhile, the ring around the Alamo tightened. Santa Anna's men were so near that Andrea could make out the words of their Spanish jokes.

On the evening of March 5, Travis called the men to a meeting in front of the Alamo church. Bowie insisted on attending. Andrea had his cot carried outside.

Travis faced the men. With the point of his sword, he drew a line in the dirt. He said, "Those who want to fight it out with me, come inside that line. Those who have had enough and think they can escape, go outside."

Andrea watched as all but two men quickly stepped across the line. "One of these two men sprang over the wall and disappeared," remembered Andrea. "The other man was Jim Bowie. He made an effort to rise, but failed, and with tears streaming from his eyes, said: 'Boys, won't none of you help me over there?'"

Crockett and several others sprang toward his cot. They carried the brave man across the line.

"We all knew we were doomed," said Andrea. "Not one of us, though, was in favor of surrendering."

That evening, many women slipped out of the Alamo. But Andrea stayed with the Alamo defenders. They would need her.

The end came suddenly and with a rush. It was hours before dawn, on March 6, when Andrea was awakened by a Mexican bugle. It was playing the first notes of the "Degüello" ("Cut-throat"). Andrea shuddered.

Colonel Travis ran across the yard, shouting, "Come on, boys, the Mexicans are upon us and we'll give 'em Hell!" The men fumbled in the darkness for their rifles.

Crockett told his boys, "I think we had better march out and die in the open air. I don't like to be hemmed up." They took their posts at the low south wall and waited.

The women led their crying children inside the church. Andrea was already in the church, at Bowie's side. "I tried to keep him as calm as possible," she said.

The Mexican army came at a run, shouting, "¡Viva, Santa Anna!" Cannon boomed. The Texans fired their rifles at the Mexican soldiers climbing over the walls on all sides. Load and fire! Load and fire! The Texans had to aim blindly, it was so dark and smoky. Hauntingly, the Degüello played on.

Andrea peered out of a small window. "It was an awful scene — Mexicans and Texans all mixed up," she remembered. "The range was too short for shooting, so they clubbed their rifles and fought hand-to-hand!"

Bowie started coughing violently. Andrea cradled his head in her arms and offered him a sip of water. Just then, a dozen Mexican soldiers pushed past the sandbags and smashed down the church doors.

"They sprang into our room," recalled Andrea. "They came at Jim with their bayonets."

She tried to protect Bowie. "I threw myself in front of him," said Andrea, "and received two bayonets in my body. One passed through my arm and another through the flesh of my chin."

She begged the soldiers not to murder a sick man. But they shoved her aside. As Colonel Jim Bowie lay in her lap, helpless and unarmed, they killed him.

The guns went silent. In less than two hours, the battle was over.

"I walked out of the room," said Andrea. "When I stepped onto the floor of the Alamo, blood ran into my shoes."

Mexican guards led her outside to the Alamo yard. The scene was terrible to behold. Strewn about were the lifeless bodies of the brave Texans.

"Although they had fought like demons," Andrea recalled, "every one of my Alamo friends was dead." The Alamo had fallen.

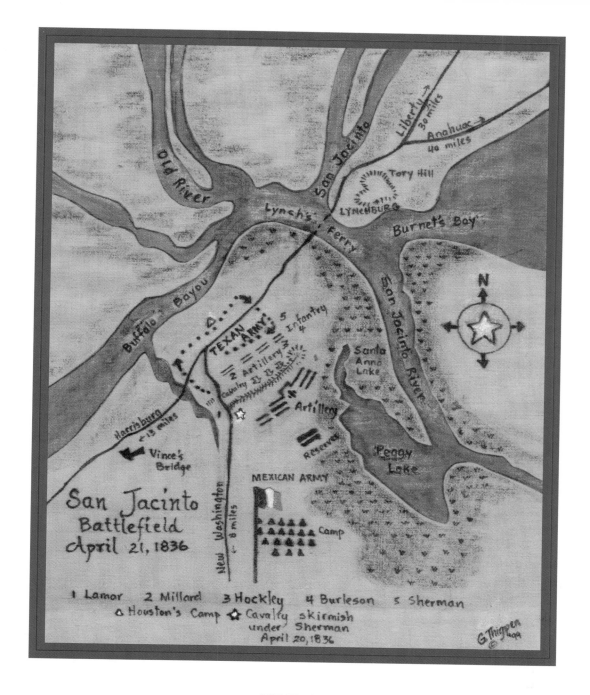

San Jacinto Battlefield April 21, 1836

1 Lamor 2 Millard 3 Hockley 4 Burleson 5 Sherman
△ Houston's Camp ✪ Cavalry skirmish under Sherman April 20, 1836

EPILOGUE

Just forty-one days after the Texans were defeated at the Alamo, the Mexican army was defeated at San Jacinto. Texas gained its independence from Mexico.

For the rest of her life, Andrea was an Angel of Mercy. When, in 1842, she heard that the bodies of fourteen Texans slain by Indians were to be buried in a common grave, she ordered the bodies brought to her. She washed them, bought shrouds and coffins, and paid for a Christian burial.

She plucked strangers off the streets and cared for them. Besides raising four of her own children, she adopted twenty-two orphans. In 1849, a group of families became stranded in San Antonio on their way to the California gold mines. She gave them cash and food and sent them on their way.

During the cholera epidemics of 1849 and 1866, she went from house-to-house tending the sick.

In 1891, the Texas Legislature granted Andrea Castañón Villanueva $150 a year in honor of her support of the Texans in their struggle for independence.

Even this money she gave away. Always in sympathy with freedom fighters, she donated money to the Cuban Revolution.

In time, Candelario died, her children moved away, and she closed the restaurant. She came to be called "Madam Candelaria." She lived alone with her fat chihuahua that kept her feet warm.

When she was an old woman, she loved to sit in the sunshine in front of the Alamo. To anyone who would listen, she recited the tragic events of 1836. She was the last survivor of the Battle of the Alamo. She was photographed, interviewed, and painted. She became quite famous.

At the age of 95, Andrea fell ill. On her deathbed, she said, "Why is it that God does not take me away when I suffer so? I have never done anyone any harm and have always tried to do good."

God must have agreed with her. These were her last words.

TEXAS 1836

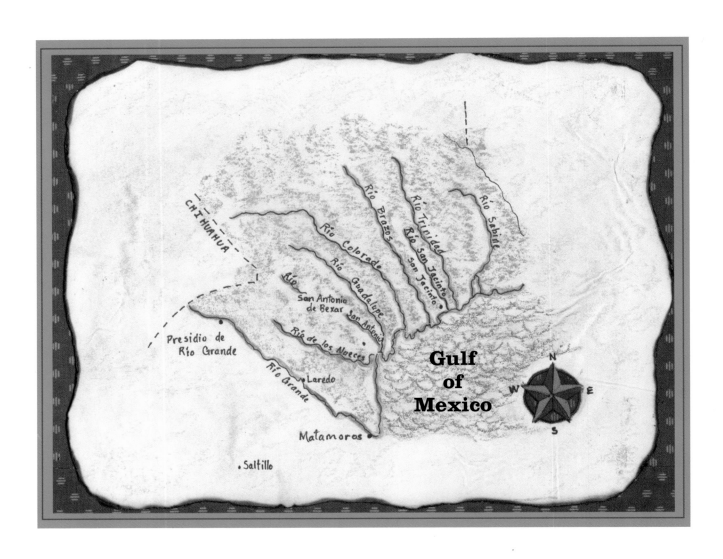

Important Dates in Texas History

1500's -1600's	The Spanish look for gold in Texas. Texas is considered dangerous and distant. Little attempt is made to colonize it.
1682	Spanish control of Texas is threatened when French explorer, Sieur de la Salle, establishes Fort St. Louis on the Texas coast.
1690's-1750's	The Spanish build missions and forts across Texas, strengthening their control.
1718	The mission San Antonio de Valero, later known as the Alamo, is founded. San Antonio de Béxar, the village that grew up around it, becomes the largest settlement in Spanish Texas. It is situated on the King's Highway, the main supply route linking Texas to Mexico.
1810	Mexicans fight for independence from Spain.
1813	Spanish troops invade San Antonio, executing suspected revolutionaries and imprisoning women.
1821	Mexico wins independence. Stephen F. Austin settles 300 American families in Texas.
1824	Mexico becomes a republic.
1833	General Antonio López de Santa Anna is elected president.
1834	President Santa Anna rejects the Constitution of 1824 and becomes a dictator.
1835	Mexican General Cós invades San Antonio. The Texas Revolution begins.
1836	The Alamo falls to Mexican forces under Santa Anna. Santa Anna's army is defeated at San Jacinto. Texas wins independence from Mexico.
1845	Texas becomes the 28th state in the U.S.A.

Index